泰戈尔写给孩子的诗

〔印〕拉宾德拉纳特·泰戈尔（Rabindranath Tagore）/文

徐翰林/译　　张王哲/图

化学工业出版社

·北京·

图书在版编目（CIP）数据

泰戈尔写给孩子的诗：中英双语美绘版 /（印）拉宾
德拉纳特·泰戈尔 (Rabindranath Tagore) 文；徐翰林译；
张王哲图. —北京：化学工业出版社，2023.8（2025.7重印）
　ISBN 978-7-122-43576-7

　Ⅰ.①泰… Ⅱ.①拉… ②徐… ③张… Ⅲ.①儿童诗歌—
散文诗—诗集—印度—现代—汉、英 Ⅳ.①I351.82

中国国家版本馆CIP数据核字（2023）第098409号

责任编辑：王婷婷　　　　　　　　　　　　　　　封面设计：李梦婷
责任校对：李雨晴　　　　　　　　　　　　　　　装帧设计：盟诺文化

出版发行：化学工业出版社（北京市东城区青年湖南街13号　邮政编码100011）
印　　装：北京建宏印刷有限公司
889mm×1194mm　1/24　印张6　字数150千字　2025年7月北京第1版第2次印刷

购书咨询：010-64518888　　　　　　　　　　　　售后服务：010-64518899
网　　址：http://www.cip.com.cn
凡购买本书，如有缺损质量问题，本社销售中心负责调换。

定　　价：38.00元

前　言

  泰戈尔，一位伟大的哲学家，一个爱国爱民之人，一位多才多艺的诗人，一生创作五十多部诗集，被授予诺贝尔文学奖。他的一生曾经历无数坎坷，却用博爱之心化解一切，让快乐在心中流淌，从指尖流出，洋溢在字里行间。

  有人曾说，他是"孩子的天使"，化身孩童，用天真稚嫩的语言，天马行空的想象力，描绘出一个美好的新月国度。

  《新月集》就是泰戈尔写给孩子的诗，它有一种神奇的魔力，其中一个个零散的故事，如同被诗人施了魔法：谁才是真正的窃眠者，去哪里能抓住他？载着我的名字和住址的纸船会飘到哪里呢？花儿在地下学校里会不会闯祸？……

  诗人为了追寻他的童年梦，一路不断变换角色，是妈妈、孩子还是本色出演？聆听这一首首时而温柔，时而调皮的诗歌，体味诗人诠释母亲与孩子之间的爱，歌颂神奇的大自然，抑或是表达人与自然的和谐相处之美。

  可以说，泰戈尔将其哲学思想注入诗歌，描绘出对生活的美好向往，展现了深邃的诗歌底蕴。现在，让我们跟着这一首首小诗走进诗歌的世界，点亮智慧人生。

泰戈尔

　　拉宾德拉纳特·泰戈尔（Rabindranath Tagore，1861 年—1941 年），印度诗人、文学家、社会活动家、哲学家和印度民族主义者。代表作有《吉檀迦利》《飞鸟集》《新月集》《家庭与世界》《园丁集》《最后的诗篇》《戈拉》《文明的危机》等。1913 年，他以《吉檀迦利》成为第一位获得诺贝尔文学奖的亚洲人。

　　泰戈尔的诗风对中国现代文学产生过重大影响，启迪了郭沫若、徐志摩、冰心等一代文豪，其中许多作品多次被译成中文。

目 录

家

我独自走在穿越田地的小路上，
夕阳像一个吝啬鬼，
正藏起它最后的一点金子。

白昼渐渐地没入深深的黑暗之中，
那收割后的田野，
孤寂、沉默地躺在那里。

突然，
一个男孩尖锐的歌声划破了天空，
他穿越看不见的黑暗，
留下他的歌声回荡在静谧的黄昏里。

他的家就在荒地边缘的村落里，
穿过甘蔗园，
隐匿在香蕉树和瘦长的槟榔树，
以及椰子树和深绿色的榴梿的阴影里。

星光下，
我独自行走着，
途中停留了片刻，
看着幽暗的大地在我面前展开，
正用她的双臂拥抱着无数的家庭，
在那里有摇篮和床铺，
有母亲们的心和夜晚的灯光，
还有年轻的生命，
自然而欢乐的，
却全然不知这欢乐对于世界的价值。

海 边

孩子们相聚在无垠世界的海边。

辽阔的穹隆在头上静止，
不息的海水在脚下汹涌澎湃。
孩子们相聚在无垠世界的海边，
欢叫着手舞足蹈。

他们用沙来筑屋，
玩弄着空空的贝壳。
他们用落叶编成船，
笑着让它们漂浮在深海里。
孩子们在世界的海边自娱自乐。

他们不懂得怎么游泳，
他们不晓得怎样撒网。
采珠的人潜水寻找宝珠，
商人在船上航行，
孩子们却把鹅卵石拾起又扔掉。

他们不找宝藏，
他们不知怎样撒网。
大海欢笑着翻腾浪花，
而海滩的微笑泛着暗淡的光。
凶险的惊涛骇浪，
对孩子们唱着没有意义的曲子，
仿佛母亲在晃悠婴儿入睡时的哼唱。

大海和孩子们一同玩耍，
而海滩的微笑泛着暗淡的光。
孩子们相聚在无垠世界的海边。
暴风骤雨在广袤的天穹中怒吼，
航船沉寂在无垠的大海里，
死亡临近，
孩子们却在玩耍。

在无垠世界的海边，
有着孩子们盛大的聚会。

004

起　源

掠过婴儿双目的睡眠，
有谁知道它来自何方？
是的，
传说它来自森林阴影中，
萤火虫迷离之光照耀着的梦幻村落，
在那儿悬挂着两个腼腆而迷人的蓓蕾。
它从那儿飞来，
轻吻着婴儿的双眸。

当婴儿沉睡时唇边闪现的微笑，
有谁知道它来自何方？
是的，
传说是新月那一丝青春的柔光，
碰触到将逝的秋云边缘，
于是微笑便乍现在沐浴露珠的清晨的梦中
——当婴儿沉睡时，
微笑便在他唇边闪现。

甜美柔嫩的新鲜气息，
如花朵般绽放在婴儿的四肢上，
——有谁知道它久久地藏匿在什么地方？
是的，
当妈妈还是少女时，
它已在她心间，
在爱的温柔和静谧的神秘中潜伏，
——甜美柔嫩的新鲜气息，
如花朵般绽放在婴儿的四肢上。

婴儿之道

只要婴儿愿意，
此刻他便可飞上天堂。
他之所以没有离开我们，
并非没有原因。
他喜欢把头靠在妈妈的怀中，
哪怕一刻没见到她都不行。
婴儿知道所有智慧的语言，
尽管世上很少有人能知晓其含义。
他之所以不愿说话，
并非没有原因。
他想做的事，
就是要学从妈妈嘴里说出来的话。
这就是为什么他看起来如此天真。

婴儿有成堆的金银珠宝，
但他却像个乞儿一样来到这个世界。
他如此伪装，并非没有原因。
这个可爱的小乞儿裸着身子，
装作完全无助的样子，

是想乞求妈妈爱的财富。
婴儿在纤细的新月之境，
自由自在，无拘无束。
他放弃自由，并非没有原因。
他知道在妈妈心房的小小角落里，
有着无穷的欢乐，
被搂在妈妈爱的臂弯里，
其甜蜜远胜于自由。

婴儿从不知怎样啼哭。
他住在极为幸福的国度里。
他流泪，并非没有原因。
虽然他那可爱的小脸儿上的微笑，
系着妈妈热切的心，
然而他因小小麻烦发出的啜泣，
却织成了怜惜与关爱的双重牵绊。

被忽略的盛会

啊，谁把那条小裙子染上了颜色，
我的孩子，
谁给你温润的四肢套上那件小红衣？
你清晨出来在院子里玩耍，
你跑得摇摇晃晃跌跌撞撞。
但究竟是谁把那条小裙子染上颜色的，
我的孩子？
什么事让你大笑，我生命的小蓓蕾？
妈妈站在门口，微笑地望着你。

她拍着手，
手镯叮当作响，
你手执竹竿跳着舞，活像一个小牧童。
但究竟什么事让你大笑，我生命的小蓓蕾？
哦，小乞儿，
你双手搂着妈妈的脖子，想要些什么？
哦，贪婪的心，
要我把整个世界从天上摘下来，
像摘果实那样，

把它放在你纤小的玫瑰色掌心里吗？
哦，小乞儿，
你在乞求什么？
风欢喜地带走了你脚踝上的叮当声。
太阳微笑着，看你梳洗。

当你在妈妈臂弯里睡觉时，
天空凝视着你，
晨光轻手轻脚地来到你床前，
轻吻你的眼睛。
风欢喜地带走了你脚踝上的叮当声。
梦中的精灵正穿越薄暮的天空向你飞来。
那世界之母借着你妈妈的心，
保留与你毗邻的位子。
他，那个为群星奏乐的人正拿着长笛站在你窗前。
梦中的精灵正穿越薄暮的天空向你飞来。

窃 眠 者

谁从婴儿的眼中窃去了睡眠？我必须知道。

妈妈把她的水壶夹在腰间，去邻村汲水。

正午时分。

孩童的戏耍时间已经结束；

池塘里的鸭子沉默无声。

牧童在榕树的树荫下睡去了。

白鹤庄严而安静地立在芒果树旁的泥沼中。

此时，窃眠者进来，

从婴儿的眼中偷走了睡眠，飞走了。

当妈妈回来时，发现婴儿在屋里的地板上爬着。

谁从婴儿的眼中窃去了睡眠？我必须知道。

我一定要找到她，把她锁起来。

我一定要去那个黑洞里查找，

在那儿，

一条小溪从圆的、有皱纹的石头中汩汩流出。

我一定要在醉花丛中氤氲的树影里寻找，

在那儿，

鸽子在它们的角落里咕咕地叫着，

精灵的脚环在繁星满空的静夜里叮当作响。

黄昏时，

我睥睨着竹林呢喃的静谧，

萤火虫在那儿挥霍着它们的光芒，

我将寻问我遇到的每一个生灵：

  "谁能告诉我窃眠者住在哪里？"

谁从婴儿的眼中窃去了睡眠？我必须知道。

我一旦抓住她，

就好好教训她一顿！

我将闯入她的窝，

看看她把窃得的睡眠藏在何处。

我将夺来她的一切，带回家。

我要牢牢锁住她的羽翼，

把她放在河边，

给她一根芦苇，

让她在灯芯草和睡莲间钓鱼嬉戏。

黄昏，街市已经收了，
村里的孩子们坐在妈妈的膝上，
于是夜鸟便在她耳边讥笑着说：
"你现在要窃谁的睡眠呢？"

开　始

"我是从哪里来的，你在哪里把我捡来的？"
孩子问他的妈妈。
她把孩子紧紧地搂在胸前，
半哭半笑地回答道：
"你曾经是我藏在心底的心愿，我的宝贝。"
"你曾藏在我儿时玩的泥娃娃身上；
每天早晨我用泥土塑造我的神像，
那时我塑造完又捏碎的就是你。"
"你曾同我们家的守护神一样被敬奉，
我敬拜家神时也就敬拜了你。"

"你曾活在我一切的希望和爱里，
活在我的生命里，活在我母亲的生命里。"
"在支配着我们家庭的不灭精神之膝上，
你已经被抚育了好几代了。"

"当我在女孩时代时，我的心如花瓣儿张开，
你就像那一股散发出的花香。"
"你的温柔在我年轻的肢体上开花了，
像一道曙光在太阳出来之前划过天空。"

"天堂里的第一个宠儿与晨曦一同降临，
你沿着世界生命的溪流漂浮而下，
终于在我的心头停泊。"
"当我凝视你的脸时，
神秘感震撼着我，
原属于一切的你，竟成了我的。"

"因为怕失去你，
我把你紧紧地拥在怀里。
是什么魔法把这世界的宝贝
牵引到我这纤弱的臂膀中的呢？"

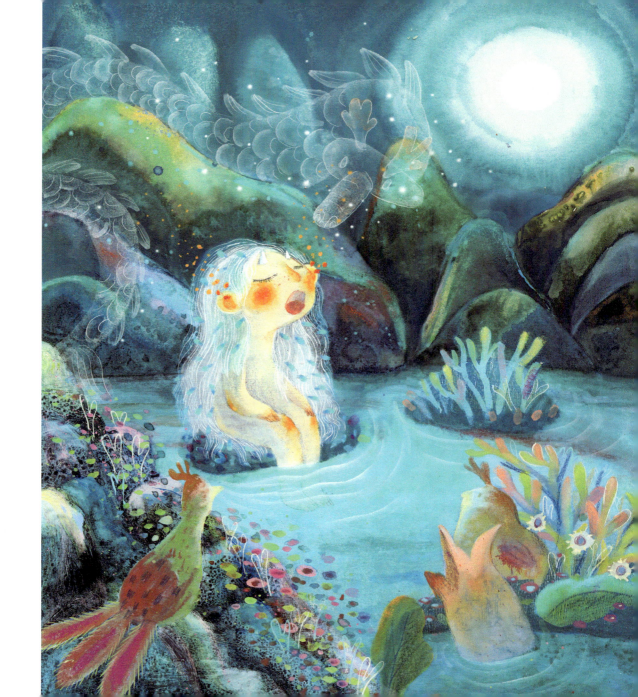

孩童的世界

我愿我能在我孩子自己的世界中占一方净土。
我知道繁星会对他私语，
天空也会俯身来到他面前，
用它傻傻的云朵和彩虹来逗弄他。

那些让人以为不会说话和看起来永不会动弹的人，
带着他们的故事和满是明亮玩具的托盘，
悄悄地爬到他的窗前。

我愿我能在穿越孩子心灵的道路上旅行，
摆脱所有的束缚；

在那里，
使者徒然奔走于没有历史的王国君主间；
在那里，
理智把她的法则当作风筝来放飞，
真理也会使事实摆脱羁绊，得以自由。

时间和原因

当我给你彩色玩具时，
我的孩子，
我明白了为什么在云端、
在水中会如此色彩斑斓，
明白了为什么花儿会被上色
——当我给你彩色玩具时，
我的孩子。

当我唱着歌使你翩翩起舞时，
我确实明白了为什么树叶会哼着乐曲，
为什么海浪将其和声传到聆听着的大地心中
——当我唱着歌使你翩翩起舞时。

当我把糖果放到你贪婪的手中时，
我明白了为什么花杯中会有蜜汁，
为什么水果里会神秘地蕴涵着甜美的果汁
——当我把糖果放到你贪婪的手中时。

当我轻吻着你的小脸使你微笑时，
我的宝贝，
我确实明白了晨光中天空流淌的是怎样的欢欣，
夏日微风吹拂在我身上是怎样的愉悦
——当我轻吻着你的小脸使你微笑时。

责　备

为什么你的眼中有泪水，
我的孩子？
他们是多么可恶，
常常无故责备你？
你写字时墨水弄脏了小手和小脸——
这就是他们说你肮脏的原因吗？
呸，
他们敢骂满月肮脏吗，
因为墨水也弄脏了它的脸？

他们总是为每一件小事责备你，
我的孩子，
他们总是平白无故地找你麻烦。
你在玩耍时不小心扯破了衣服——

这就是他们说你邋遢的原因吗？
呸，
那从破碎的云翳中露出微笑的秋之晨，
他们要怎么说呢？

别去理睬他们对你说什么，
我的孩子。
他们将你的错误行径罗列了一长串。
谁都知道你特别喜欢糖果——
这就是他们说你贪婪的原因吗？
呸，
那我们如此喜爱你，
他们要怎么说呢？

法 官

你想说他什么就尽情地说吧，
但我了解我孩子的缺点。

我不是因为他好才爱他的，
只是因为他是我的小宝贝。

如果你只是衡量他的优缺点，
你怎会明白他是多么的可爱？

当我必须惩罚他时，
他更成为我生命中的一部分了。

当我让他流泪时，
我的心也跟着一起哭泣。

只有我才有权去责罚他，
因为只有深爱他的人才可以惩戒他。

玩　具

孩子，

整个早晨你那么快乐地坐在泥土里，

玩着折断的小树枝儿。

我微笑着看你玩那根折断的小树枝儿。

我正忙着算账，

一小时一小时地累积着数字。

或许你看我一眼，

想："这种无聊的游戏，竟毁了你整个早晨！"

孩子，我已忘了一心一意玩树枝儿与泥饼的方法了。

我寻求贵重的玩具，

收集大把的金银。

无论你找到什么，

总能创造使你快乐的游戏，

我却把时间和精力消磨在我永远得不到的东西上。

在我单薄的独木舟里，

我挣扎着要横穿欲望之海，

竟忘了自己也在其中游戏。

天文学家

我只不过说：

"当黄昏圆圆的满月缠绕在昙花枝头时，

难道没有人能捉住它吗？"

哥哥笑着对我说：

"孩子啊，你真是我所见过的最傻的孩子。

月亮离我们如此远，谁能捉住它呢？"

我说："哥哥，你才傻呢！

当妈妈望着窗外，

微笑着俯视我们嬉戏时，你能说她离我们远吗？"

哥哥又说："你这傻孩子！

可是，孩子啊，

你到哪里才能找到一张大得足以捉住月亮的网呢？"

我说："当然，你可以用双手去捉住它呀。"

但是哥哥还是笑着说：

"你真是我所见过的最傻的孩子！

如果月亮近了，你就知道它有多大了。"

我说："哥哥，

你们学校里教的，真是一派胡言！

当妈妈俯下脸亲吻我们时，

她的脸看起来也是非常大吗？"

但哥哥还是说："你真是个傻孩子。"

云 与 浪

妈妈,
那些住在云端的人对我喊道——
"我们从早晨醒来玩到天黑。
我们与金色的曙光嬉戏,
我们与皎洁的月亮嬉戏。"
我问:"但是,我怎样才能到你那里呢?"

他们回答说:
"你到大地的边缘来,对着天空举起双手,
就会被接上云端。"
"我妈妈在家里等我呢,"我说,
"我怎能离她而去呢?"
于是他们微笑着飘走了。

但是,妈妈,
我知道一个比这个更好玩的游戏。
我做云,你做月亮。
我用双手遮住你,
我们的屋顶就是湛蓝的天空。

那些住在波浪上的人对我喊道——
"我们从一早唱歌直到晚上;
我们不停地前进旅行,
不知将要经过什么地方。"
我问:"但是,
我怎样才能加入到你们的队伍中呢?"

他们告诉我:"来到海边,
紧闭双眼站在那里,
你就被带到波浪上来了。"
我说:
"黄昏时,妈妈常常要我待在家里——
我怎能离她而去呢?"
于是他们笑着,舞着,离去了。

但是我知道一个比这更好玩的游戏。
我做波浪,你做陌生的岸。
我奔腾前进,大笑着撞碎在你的膝上。
世上没有人知道我们俩在什么地方。

金色花

如果我变成了一朵金色花，
仅仅为了好玩，
长在那高高的枝头，
笑着摇曳在风中，
又舞动在新生的叶上，
妈妈，你会认得我吗？
你若是叫道："宝贝，你在哪儿？"
我偷偷地笑，不发出一点声音。
我会静静地绽放花瓣，看着你工作。

当你沐浴完毕，
湿湿的头发散在两肩，
穿过金色花的树影，
走到你做祷告的小庭院时，
你会闻到这花儿的香气，
却不知这香气是从我身上散发出来的。

当午饭后，
你坐在窗前读《罗摩衍那》，
那棵树的阴影落到你的头发与膝盖之间，
我会在你的书页上，
就在你正读着的地方投下我的稚影。
可是你会猜到这就是你的小孩的稚影吗？

当黄昏时，
你拿着灯去牛棚，
于是，我突然又落到地上，
再变成你的孩子，
要你讲个故事给我听。
"你去哪儿了，你这淘气的孩子？"
"我不告诉你，妈妈。"
这便是我和你要说的话。

【注】《罗摩衍那》：意思为"罗摩的历险经历"，与《摩诃婆罗多》并列为印度两大史诗，作者是印度作家蚁垤（跋弥）。

仙　境

假如人们知道我的国王的宫殿在哪里，
它便会在空气中消失。
墙壁是白银，房顶是璀璨的黄金。

王后住在有七个庭院的宫殿里，
她戴着一串珠宝，整整值七个王国的财富。

不过，妈妈，
让我偷偷告诉你，
我的国王的宫殿到底在哪里。
它就在我们阳台的一隅，
在那放着种植杜尔茜花盆的地方。

在遥远的、不可逾越的七重海岸的那一边，
公主沉睡着。
除了我，世上没有人能找到她。
她臂上戴着镯子，耳上悬着珍珠；
她的头发长得拖在地板上。

当我用我的魔杖触碰她时，
她便会醒来；
而当她微笑时，珠宝会从她唇边滑落。
不过，让我偷偷地对你耳语，
妈妈，她就在我们阳台的一隅，
在那放着种植杜尔茜花盆的地方。

当你去河里沐浴时，你走上屋顶的阳台。
我就坐在那墙头阴影聚集的角落里。
跟我在一起的只有小猫咪，
因为它清楚故事中的理发师居住的地方。

不过，让我偷偷地对你耳语，
妈妈，那故事里的理发师住在哪里。
他居住的地方就在阳台的一隅，
在那放着种植杜尔茜花盆的地方。

流放之地

妈妈，天空中的光成了灰色，
我不知道是什么时间了。
我的游戏挺无趣的，于是过来找你。
这是星期六，我们的节日。
放下你的活儿，妈妈，
靠在窗的一边坐着，
告诉我童话里的特潘塔沙漠在哪儿？
整整一天都在被雨的影子覆盖着。
凶猛的闪电用利爪抓着天空。

当乌云发出雷鸣的时候，
我喜欢怀着恐惧紧紧依偎在你身上；
当倾盆大雨几个小时不停地拍打着竹叶，
而我们的窗户被狂风刮得嘎吱作响的时候，
我喜欢单独和你坐在屋里，
妈妈，听你讲童话里的特潘塔沙漠的故事。

它在哪里，妈妈？

在哪一个海岸上，

在哪一座山脚下，

在哪一个国王的疆土上？

田野上没有篱笆来标明界线，

也没有一条穿越田野的小径，

让村人在黄昏时走回村落，

或者让在树林中拾干柴的妇人将柴带往市场。

沙漠上只有小丛小丛的黄草和一棵树，

上面有一对聪明的老鸟搭建的窝，

那个地方就是特潘塔沙漠。

我能够想象得出，

在这样一个阴云密布的日子，

国王那年轻的儿子，

怎样独自骑着一匹灰马，

穿越这沙漠，

横渡不知名的海洋，

寻找那被巨人囚禁的公主。

当雨雾在遥远的天空下沉，

闪电犹如一阵突发的痛苦痉挛出现时，

他是否还记得，
当他骑马穿越童话里的特潘塔沙漠时，
他那不幸的母亲被国王抛弃，
正含着泪水清扫牛棚？
看，妈妈，一天还没过去，天色几乎都黑了，
村庄那边的路上已没什么游人了。
牧童早就从牧场上回家了，
人们也已从田地归来，
坐在他们屋檐下的草席上，
望着阴沉的云层。

妈妈，我把所有的书都放上书架了——现在别让我做功课。
当我长大了，
像爸爸一样大的时候，
我会掌握必须学的东西。
但是今天，请告诉我，妈妈，
童话里的特潘塔沙漠在什么地方？

雨　天

乌云迅速地聚集在森林那黑暗的边缘上。
　喔，孩子，不要出去！
湖边一排棕榈树，
正把头撞向阴沉的天空；
羽毛凌乱的乌鸦，
悄然栖息在罗望子的枝上，
河的东岸萦绕着浓浓的忧郁。
我们拴在篱笆上的牛正高声鸣叫着。

喔，孩子，在这里等着，
等我把牛牵进棚里。
人们都挤在清水流溢的田间，
捉那些从漫出的池水中逃出来的鱼儿；
雨水涨成了溪流，
流过狭小的巷子，
像一个嬉闹的孩子从他妈妈身边跑开，
故意惹怒她似的。
听，有人在渡口喊船夫呢。

　喔，孩子，天色昏暗，
渡口的渡船已经停了。
天空像疾驰在滂沱的雨中；
河水暴躁地喧嚣着；
女人们早已从恒河畔汲满了水，
带着水罐匆匆回家去了。

夜晚用的灯，一定要准备好。
　喔，孩子，不要出去！

去市场的大道已无人行走，
去河边的小径很滑。

风在竹林里咆哮挣扎着，
好像一只落入陷阱的野兽。

纸　　船

我每天把纸船一只只地放入急流中。
我在纸船上用大而黑的字写着我的名字和我住的村名。
我期盼着住在异乡的人会发现它们，
知道我是谁。

我在小船上放着花园里长的雪莉花，
希望这些在拂晓时分开放的花能在夜里被平安地带上岸。
我把我的纸船投进水里，
仰望天空，
看见小小的云朵正扬起鼓满了风的白帆。
我不知道，
天上的哪个玩伴把这些船送下来和我的船比赛！

夜幕降临，
我把脸埋在手臂里，
梦见我的纸船在午夜的星空下漂浮前行。
睡仙坐在船里，
带着满载着梦的篮子。

水　手

船夫马杜的船在拉耿尼码头停泊着。
这只船载着废弃的黄麻，
已经长久地闲置在那里。
只要他乐意把船借给我，
我会给它装上一百只桨，
扬起五个、六个或七个风帆来。
我决不把它驶进愚蠢的集市。

我将到仙境里的七大洋和十三条河中航行。
但是，妈妈，
不要躲在角落里为我哭泣。
我不会像罗摩犍陀罗一样，
去森林里，一去十四年才回来。

我将成为故事中的王子，
让我的船装满我喜欢的所有东西。
我将带我的朋友阿苏与我同行，
我们要快快乐乐地在仙境里的七大洋和十三条河中航行。

我们将在晨曦中扬帆航行。
午间，
你正在池塘里沐浴时，
我们将在一个陌生的国度中。

我们将经过特浦尼浅滩，
把特潘塔沙漠远远丢在我们身后。

当我们回来时，
天色渐黑，
我将告诉你我们所看见的一切。
我将穿越仙境里的七大洋和十三条河。

对 岸

我渴望到那边，到河的对岸。
在那里，
那些小船排成一行系在竹竿上；
清晨，人们乘船到那边去，
肩上扛着锄头，到他们远处的田中去耕耘。
在那边，
放牛的人赶着鸣叫的牛涉水到对岸的牧场；
黄昏时分，他们都回家了，
只留下豺狼在这长满野草的岛上哀嚎。
妈妈，如果你不介意，
我长大后，要当这渡船的船夫。

有人说在这个高岸的后面藏着许多古怪的池塘。
雨过后，一群群野鸭飞到那里去，
茂盛的芦苇长满了池塘四周，
水鸟在那里生蛋，竹鸡摇着会跳舞的尾巴，
在洁净的软泥上印下它们细小的足印；
黄昏时，长草顶着白花，
邀月光在它们的波浪上荡漾。

妈妈，如果你不介意，
我长大后，要当这渡船的船夫。
我要从此岸到彼岸，来回摆渡，
村里所有正在沐浴的男孩女孩，
都会惊奇地望着我。
太阳升到半空，清晨变为正午，
我会跑到你那里去，
说："妈妈，我饿了！"
一天结束了，影子俯伏在树底下，
我会在黄昏时回家。
我一定不会像爸爸那样，
离开你到城里去工作。
妈妈，如果你不介意，
我长大后，一定要当这渡船的船夫。

花的学校

当乌云在天空轰鸣，
六月的阵雨落下时，
湿润的东风吹过荒野，
在竹林间奏响它的风笛。
突然，
成簇的花朵从无人知晓的地方跑来，
在绿草上跳舞狂欢。

妈妈，
我真的认为那成簇的花是在地下的学校里上学。
他们关门闭户做功课，
如果他们想在放学之前出来玩耍，
他们的老师就会让他们在墙角罚站。

一下雨，他们就放假了。
树枝在林中交错，
叶子在狂风中簌簌作响，
雷雨云拍着它们的巨手，
小花们就身穿粉的、黄的、白的衣裳，冲了出来。

你知道吗？
妈妈，
他们的家是在天上，
在星星居住的地方。
你没有看见他们怎样地急着要去那儿？
你难道不知道他们为什么那样匆忙吗？

当然，
我可以猜出他们是为谁张开双臂：
他们也有他们的妈妈，
就像我有自己的妈妈。

商 人

妈妈，想象一下，
你待在家里，我要去异乡旅行。
再想象一下，
我的船已在码头等待起航，
船上满载货物。
现在，妈妈，
好好想想再告诉我，
我回来时要给你带些什么。

妈妈，你想要成堆的黄金吗？
那么，在黄金河的两岸，
田野里都是金黄色的稻谷。
在林荫道上，
香柏花一朵朵地飘到地上。
我将为你而收集它们，
放进数以百计的篮子里。

妈妈，你想要大如秋天雨点的珍珠吗？
我将到珍珠岛的海岸上去。
在那里的晨曦中，
珍珠在草地的花朵上颤抖，
落到草地上，
被狂野的海浪一把一把地撒在沙滩上。
我将送哥哥一匹长翅膀的马，
能在云端飞翔。
我要送爸爸一支有魔力的笔，
在他还没察觉时，
就能把字写出来。
至于你，妈妈，
我一定要送给你那个价值七个王国的
首饰盒和珠宝。

同 情

假如我只是一只小狗，
而不是你的小孩，
亲爱的妈妈，
当我想吃你盘里的东西时，
你会对我说"不"吗？
你是不是会把我赶开，
对我说："滚开，你这不听话的小狗。"
那么，走吧，
妈妈，走吧！
当你呼唤我时，
我再也不到你那里去了，
也永远不再要你喂我东西吃了。

如果我只是一只绿色的小鹦鹉，
而不是你的小孩，
亲爱的妈妈，
你会把我紧紧地拴住，怕我飞走吗？
你是不是会对我指指点点地说：

"真是一个不领情的小鸟呀！
只知道整天整夜地啄它的链子。"
那么，走吧，
妈妈，走吧！
我要到树林里去，
我决不再让你抱我入怀了。

职　业

清晨的钟敲了十下，
我沿着我们的小巷到学校去。
我每天都遇见那个小贩，
他叫着："手镯，亮晶晶的手镯！"
他没有什么急事要做，
没有哪条街道非去不可，
也没有什么时间非要回家。
我希望我是一个小贩，
整日在街上混日子，
叫着："手镯，亮晶晶的手镯！"

下午四点，我放学回家。
我从一家门口看见一个园丁在那里掘土。
他用他的锄头，想怎么挖，便怎么挖，
他的衣服落上了尘土，
如果他被太阳晒黑了或是被雨淋湿了，
没有人会骂他。
我希望我是一个园丁，
在花园里掘土，
没有人来阻止我。

天一黑，妈妈就送我上床睡觉。
我从敞开的窗口看见更夫走来走去。
小巷漆黑冷清，
路灯就像一个脸上长着一只红眼睛的
巨人立在那里。
更夫摇着他的灯笼，
他的影子随之一起移动，
他一生从没有上床歇息过。
我希望我是一个更夫，
整晚在街上行走，
提了灯笼去追逐影子。

053

长　者

妈妈，你的孩子真傻！
她是如此的孩子气！
她不知道路灯和星星的区别。

当我们玩着把石子当成食物的游戏时，
她竟以为它们是可以吃的食物，想放到嘴里去。

当我在她面前翻开一本书，
让她学 a、b、c 时，
她却用手把书页撕破，
莫名其妙地高兴地叫起来，
你的孩子就是这样做功课的。

当我生气地对她摇摇头，
责骂她，说她调皮时，
她却哈哈大笑，觉得很有趣。

所有人都知道爸爸不在家，
然而，假如我在游戏时大叫一声"爸爸"，
她会兴奋地四处张望，
以为爸爸果真就在旁边。

当我把洗衣工用来载衣服的驴子当作学生，
并且警告她说，我是校长，
她会无端地尖叫，叫我哥哥。

你的孩子想要捉住月亮。
她是如此有趣；
她把格尼许称为琪奴许。

妈妈，你的孩子真傻！
她是如此的孩子气！

【注】格尼许：是毁灭之神湿婆的儿子，象头人身。同时也是现代印度人最喜欢用来作名字的第一个字。

小 大 人

我人很小，因为我是一个小孩，

到了像我爸爸一样的年龄时，我就会变大了。

我的老师会走过来说：

"时间不早了，去把你的石板和书拿来。"

我会告诉他：

"你难道不知道我已经和爸爸一样大了吗？

我再也不做什么功课了。"

我的老师将惊讶地说：

"他不喜欢读书就不读书，因为他是大人了。"

我给自己穿好衣裳，走到人群拥挤的集市里去。

我的叔叔会跑过来说：

"你会迷路的，我的孩子；让我牵着你。"

我会告诉他：

"你看不见吗，叔叔，我已经和爸爸一样大了？

我得一个人去集市。"

叔叔将会说道：

"是的，他喜欢去哪儿就去哪儿，因为他是大人了。"

当我正拿钱给我的保姆时，

妈妈从沐浴处归来，

因为我知道如何用我的钥匙去开钱箱。

妈妈会问：

"你在做什么，淘气的孩子？"

我会告诉她：

"妈妈，你难道不知道我已经和爸爸一样大了吗？我

得拿钱给保姆。"

妈妈将自言自语地说：

"他喜欢把钱给谁就给谁，因为他是大人了。"

在十月的假期里，

爸爸将要回家，

他以为我还是个小孩子，

从城里给我带了小鞋子和小绸衫。

我会告诉他：

"爸爸，把这些东西给哥哥吧，

因为我已经和你一样大了。"

爸爸将会想一下，然后说：

"他喜欢给自己买衣衫就去买吧，因为他是大人了。"

十二点钟

妈妈，我现在不想做功课。
我已经读了整整一上午的书了。

你说，现在才十二点钟。
就算现在没有超过十二点吧，
你就不能把刚刚十二点想成下午吗？

我可以很容易就想象出：
此刻，太阳已经照到那片稻田的边缘了，
那个年迈的渔妇正在池边采撷草叶作为她的晚餐。

我一闭上眼就能想到，
马塔尔树下的阴影愈发深邃了，
池塘里的水看起来黝黑发亮。

如果十二点钟能在夜晚来临，
为什么黑夜不能在十二点钟的时候到来呢？

作 者

你说爸爸写了很多书，
可是我看不懂他写的东西。
整个黄昏他都在读书给你听，
可是你真的明白他的意思吗？

妈妈，你给我们讲的故事，多么好听啊！
我纳闷，为什么爸爸不能写那样的书呢？
难道他从来没有听过自己的妈妈讲巨人、
精灵和公主的故事吗？
还是他已经把那些故事彻底遗忘了？

他经常很晚才沐浴，
你还得去叫他一百多次。
你等候着，为他把饭菜保温，
但他总是继续写作，忘记一切。
爸爸常常视写书为游戏。

每当我走进爸爸的房里去玩耍，
你总会过来说我：
"真是个调皮的孩子啊！"

每当我稍微弄出一点声响，
你就会说：
"你难道没有看见爸爸正在工作吗？"
爸爸写呀写，有什么乐趣呢？

当我拿起爸爸的钢笔或铅笔，
像他一样在他的书上写着：
a，b，c，d，e，f，g，h，i……
你为什么对我生气呢，妈妈？
在爸爸写时，你从未说过一句。

当爸爸耗费了那么一大堆纸时，
妈妈，你好像一点都不在乎。
然而，如果我只拿出一张纸做一只船，
你却说："孩子，你真烦！"

爸爸把黑点子涂满了纸的两面，
浪费了许多纸，
你是怎样想的呢？

坏 邮 差

你为什么坐在地板上一声不吭，
告诉我啊，亲爱的妈妈?
雨从敞开的窗口飞溅进来，
把你淋透了，你却不在乎。

你听到钟已经敲了四下吗?
正是哥哥放学回家的时候。
究竟发生了什么事，你看起来如此奇怪?

你今天没有收到爸爸的信吗?
我看见邮差的袋子里装了好多信，
几乎镇上的每个人都收到信了。

只有爸爸的信，他留给自己看。
我想这个邮差是个坏人。

但是不要因此闷闷不乐，
亲爱的妈妈。
明天是邻村集市的日子。

你叫女仆去买些纸和笔回来。
我自己来写爸爸所写的每一封信;
让你找不出一点差错。
我将从 A 一直写到 K。

但是，妈妈，你为什么笑?
你不相信我会写得和爸爸一样好!
但是我将用心画线，
把所有的字母写得又大又好看。

当我写完后，
你以为我会像爸爸那样笨，
把它放到那可恶邮差的袋子里吗?
我会马上自己为你送信，
然后逐字逐句地给你读。
我知道那个邮差不愿意把真正的好信送给你。

英　雄

妈妈，我们假设一下我们正在旅行，
经过一个陌生而危险的国度。
你坐在一顶轿子里，我骑着一匹红马，跟在你身旁。
黄昏时，太阳落山。
暗淡的约拉迪希荒地在我们面前展开。
大地贫瘠而荒凉。
你害怕地想着——"我不知道我们到了什么地方了。"
　我对你说："妈妈，不要害怕。"

草原上长满了针尖般刺人的草，
一条崎岖的小径穿越其间。
在这片广袤的原野上看不见牛群，
它们已经回到村子的牛棚里了。

夜幕降临，大地和天空一片朦胧昏暗，
我们说不出我们正走向何方。
突然，你叫我，悄悄地问我：
　"靠近河岸的是什么光亮？"
正在那时，一阵可怕的号叫声传来，
一些人影向我们跑来。

你蹲在轿子里，

反复不断地祷告着神的名字。

轿夫们吓得瑟瑟发抖，

在荆棘丛中躲藏起来。

我向你喊着："不要害怕，妈妈，有我在这儿。"

他们手执长棒，

头发凌乱，越来越近了。

我大喊："小心些！你们这些坏蛋！

再往前一步，你们就等死吧。"

他们又发出可怕的号叫，冲上前来。

你紧握住我的手，说：

"乖孩子，看在上天的分儿上，离他们远些。"

我说："妈妈，看我的。"

于是我策马飞奔，

剑和盾互相撞击，铿锵作响。

这场战斗是多么激烈，

妈妈，如果你从轿子里看得见，

你一定会打冷战的。

他们中有许多人逃走了，大多数被砍成了碎片。

我知道你正独自坐在那儿，

心想，你的孩子此时肯定死了。

然而我跑到你的跟前，浑身溅满了血，

说："妈妈，战争已经结束了。"

你从轿子里走出来，

吻着我，把我搂入你的怀中，

自言自语地说：

"如果没有我的孩子保护着我，我真不知如何是好。"

日复一日，上千件无聊的事发生着，

为什么这种事就不能偶尔实现呢？

就像一本书里的故事。

我哥哥将会说：

"这怎么可能？我常常想，他是那么单薄！"

我们村里的人们都会惊讶地说：

"这孩子正和他妈妈在一起，不是很幸运吗？"

结 束

是我离开的时候了，
妈妈，我走了。
当清晨孤寂的破晓时分，
你在幽暗中伸出双臂，
想抱起你睡在床上的孩子时，
我会说："孩子不在那里了！"
——妈妈，我走了。
我将化为一缕清风爱抚着你；
我将化为串串涟漪，
当你沐浴时，
一次次地吻着你。

在刮风的夜里，
当雨点在树叶上滴答作响时，
你在床上将听到我的私语，
当电光从开着的窗口闪进你的屋里时，
我的笑声也随之一起闪现。
如果你清醒地躺在床上，
在深夜仍想着你的孩子，

我将在星空对你吟唱：
"睡吧！妈妈，睡吧。"
乘着四处游移的月光，
我悄悄地来到你床上，
趁你睡着时，躺在你怀里。
我将变成一个梦，
从你眼皮的微缝中，
滑入你的睡眠深处；
当你醒来，惊奇地张望时，
我就像一只熠熠闪光的萤火虫，
向黑暗中飞去了。

普耶节时，
当邻居的孩子们来屋里游玩时，
我将融合在笛声里，
终日荡漾在你心头。
亲爱的阿姨带了节日礼物来，
她会问道：
"我们的孩子在哪里，姐姐？"
妈妈，你要温柔地告诉她：
"他此刻在我的眼眸里，
在我的身体里，在我的灵魂里。"

呼　唤

她离开时，夜一片漆黑，他们都睡了。
这会儿，夜也一片漆黑，
我呼唤着她："回来，我的宝贝。
世界在沉睡，当繁星两两相望时，
你回来一会儿是没有人知道的。"

她离开时，草木吐芽，春意正浓。
这会儿，花儿正怒放，
我呼唤着："回来，我的宝贝。
孩子们毫无顾忌地在游戏中把花儿聚散离合，
你若回来，
带走一朵小花，没有人会发现的。"

那些常常嬉戏的人，
还在那里玩，生命就这样被荒废了。

我聆听着他们的闲聊，
呼唤着："回来，我的宝贝。
妈妈的心里充满着爱，

你若回来，
只从她那里取得一个小小的吻，没有人会妒忌的。"

最初的茉莉

啊，这些茉莉花，
这些洁白的茉莉花！

我依稀记得我的双手第一次捧满了这些茉莉花，
这些洁白的茉莉花的时候。

我曾爱那阳光，
爱那天空和那绿色的大地；
我曾在漆黑的午夜聆听那河水淙淙的呢喃。
秋日的夕阳，在荒原道路的转弯处迎接我，
好像新娘掀起她的面纱迎接她的爱人。

然而，
我回忆起孩提时第一次捧在手里的洁白茉莉花，
心里充满了甜蜜的回忆。
我平生有过许多快乐的日子，
在节日盛典的夜晚，
我曾与狂欢者一同大笑。

在细雨霏霏的清晨，
我吟唱过许多闲散的歌谣。

我颈上也曾戴着爱人用醉花亲手编织的黄昏花环。

然而，
我回忆起孩提时第一次捧在手里的洁白茉莉花，
心里充满了甜蜜的回忆。

榕　树

喂，立在池边的枝叶蓬乱的榕树，
你是否已经忘了那个小孩，
那宛如曾在你枝头筑巢，
而又离开了你的鸟儿似的小孩？

你还记得他怎样坐在窗前，
诧异地望着你那盘绕在地下的树根吗？

女人们常到池边装上满满一罐子水，
于是，你巨大的黑影在水面上荡漾，
宛如沉睡的人要挣扎着醒过来。

阳光在微波上舞动，
好似不能歇息片刻的梭子在编织着金黄的壁毯。

两只鸭子在水草边游荡，
影子在上面摇晃，
孩子静静地坐在那里沉思。
他想变成风，
吹过你簌簌的枝丫；
想变成你的影子，
随阳光在水面上消长；
想成为一只鸟儿，
栖息在你最高的枝头上；
还想变成那两只鸭，
在水草与影子中穿梭。

祝　福

祝福这颗小小的心灵，
这个纯洁的灵魂，
他为我们的大地，
赢得了上天的亲吻。
他爱阳光，他爱看妈妈的脸。

他还没学会鄙夷尘埃而追求黄金。
将他紧紧地拥抱在你的心里，并且祝福他。

他已来到这个歧路横生的大地上了。
我不知道他怎样从人群中把你挑出来，
来到你的门前握住你的手问路。
他紧随着你，说着，笑着，没有一丝疑心。
不要辜负他的信任，
引导他走向正路，并且祝福他。

将你的手轻轻按在他的头上，祈祷着：
虽然下面波涛汹涌，

然而从上面来的风，
会扬起他的船帆，
将他送到平安的港口。
不要在忙碌中把他遗忘，
让他来到你的心里，并且祝福他。

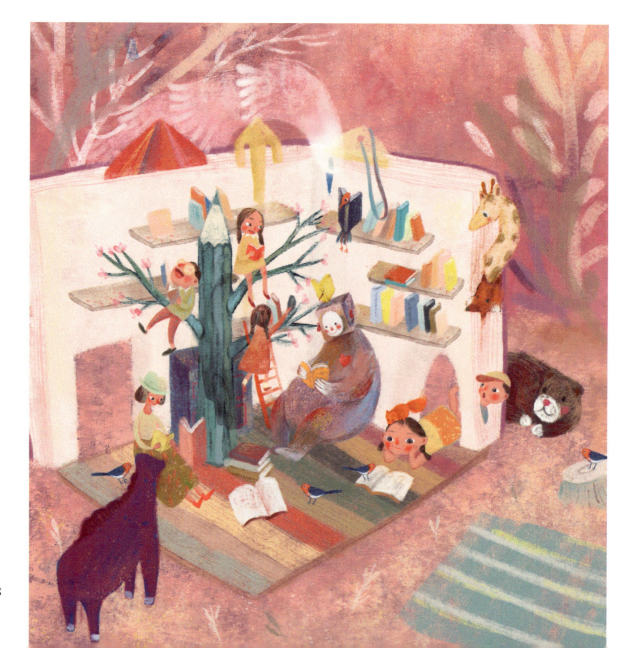

礼　物

我想送你些东西，我的孩子，
因为我们都在世界的溪流中漂泊。

我们的生命会被分开，
我们的爱也会被遗忘。

但我却没有那样傻，
指望能用我的礼物来收买你的心。

你的生命正当年轻，
你的路还很漫长，
你饮尽我们给你的爱，
就转身离开我们了。

你有你的游戏、你的玩伴。
如果你没有时间和我们在一起，
或者你不曾想到我们，那又有什么伤害呢？

在我们年老时，
自然会有许多闲暇时间，
去细数那往昔的时光，
把从我们手中永久失去的东西，
放在心里好好珍藏。

河水唱着歌奔流而去，
冲破所有的堤防。
然而山峰却留在那里追忆着，
依依不舍地跟随着她。

我 的 歌

我的孩子，
我这支歌将扬起悠扬的乐声在你的身边萦绕，
犹如那炽烈的爱之臂膀。

我这支歌将抚摸你的前额，
犹如那祝福的亲吻。

当你独处时，
它会坐在你身旁，在你耳边私语；
当你在人群中，
它会围绕着你，使你远离尘嚣。

我的歌将成为你梦想的羽翼，
它将载着你的心到那未知的边缘。
当黑夜遮蔽了你的路时，
它又成为照耀在头上的忠实星光。

我的歌将伫立在你的瞳孔里，
把你的视线植入万物心中，
当我的声音在死亡中沉寂时，
我的歌仍会在你年轻的心中吟唱。

小小天使

他们喧闹争吵，
他们猜疑失望，
他们争辩着却总是没有结果。

让你的生命融到他们中吧，我的孩子，
就像一束明亮的光芒，
使他们欢悦而静谧。

他们的贪婪和嫉妒是残酷的；
他们的言语，
如暗藏的刀，
渴望着饮血。

去，站在他们盛怒的心中，我的孩子，
把你那和善的目光投到他们身上，
仿佛那夜晚的宽容的和平遮蔽了白日的纷扰。

我的孩子，让他们看看你的脸，
于是他们明白了万物的意义；
让他们爱你，
于是他们能够相爱。

来，坐在无垠的怀抱里，我的孩子。
日出时，将心敞开，孕育成花儿；
夕阳西沉时，低下你的头，
静静地完成这一天的膜拜。

最后的交易

清晨，
我走在石头路上，
叫着："来雇用我！"
国王手执利剑乘着战车驾临。

他抓住我的手说："我用权势来雇用你。"
然而他的权势一文不值，
于是，他乘着战车离去。

炎热的正午，家家户户都关门闭户。
我漫游在蜿蜒的小巷中。
一位老者带了一袋黄金走出来。
他思索了一下，
说："我用金钱来雇用你。"
他一个一个地称着他的金币，
我却转身离去。

黄昏，花园的篱笆上繁花似锦。
漂亮的姑娘走出来，
说："我用微笑来雇用你。"
她的笑容黯淡，消失在泪痕中，
她孤单地转身走回黑暗里。

阳光照在沙滩上，
海浪随意地泼溅水花。
一个孩子坐在那里玩着贝壳。
他抬起头，好像认识我一样，
说："我雇用你，什么都不用。"

从此以后，
在这个孩子的游戏中完成的交易，
让我成了一个自由的人。

进入英文版 》》》》

THE HOME

I paced alone on the road across the field while the
sunset was hiding its last gold like a miser.

The daylight sank deeper and deeper into the darkness,
and the widowed land,
whose harvest had been reaped,
lay silent.

Suddenly a boy's shrill voice rose into the sky.
He traversed the dark unseen,
leaving the track of his song across the hush of the
evening.

His village home lay there at the end of the waste land,
beyond the sugar-cane field,
hidden among the shadows of the banana and the
slender arecapalm,
the cocoa-nut and the dark green jack-fruit trees.

I stopped for a moment in my lonely way under
the starlight,
and saw spread before me the darkened earth
surrounding with her arms countless homes
furnished with cradles and beds,
mothers' hearts and evening lamps,
and young lives glad with a gladness that knows
nothing of its value for the world.

ON THE SEASHORE

On the seashore of endless worlds children meet.
The infinite sky is motionless overhead and the
restless water is boisterous.
On the seashore of endless worlds the children meet
with shouts and dances.

They build their houses with sand,
and they play with empty shells.
With withered leaves they weave their boats and
smilingly float them on the vast deep.
Children have their play on the seashore of worlds.

They know not how to swim,
they know not how to cast nets.
Pearl—fishers dive for pearls,
merchants sail in their ships,
while children gather pebbles and scatter them again.
They seek not for hidden treasures,
they know not how to cast nets.

The sea surges up with laughter,
and pale light gleams the smile of the
seabeach.
Death—dealing waves sing meaningless
ballads to the children,
even like the lullaby while rocking her
baby's cradle.
The sea plays with children,
and pale light gleams the smile of the
seabeach.

On the seashore of endless worlds children
meet.
Tempest roams in the pathless sky,
ships are wrecked in the trackless water,
death is abroad and children play.
On the seashore of endless worlds is the
great meeting of children.

THE SOURCE

The sleep that flits on baby's eyes,

does anybody know from where it comes?

Yes,

there is a rumor that it has its dwelling where,

 in the fairy village among shadows of the

forest dimly lit with glowworms,

there hang two shy buds of enchantment.

From there it comes to kiss baby's eyes.

The smile that flickers on baby's lips when he

sleeps,

does anybody know where it was born?

Yes,

there is a rumor that a young soft beam

of a crescent moon touched the edge of a

vanishing autumn cloud,

and there the smile was first born in the

dream of a dew—washed morning—the smile

that flickers on baby's lips when he sleeps.

The sweet, soft freshness that blooms

on baby's limbs —does anybody know

where it was hidden so long?

Yes,

when the mother was a young girl it

lay pervading her heart in tender and

silent mystery of love —the sweet,

soft freshness that has bloomed on

baby's limbs.

BABY'S WAY

If only baby wanted to,
he could fly up to heaven this moment.
It is not for nothing that he does not leave us.
He loves to rest his head on mother's bosom,
and cannot ever bear to lose sight of her.
Baby knows all manner of wise words, though few
on earth can understand their meaning.
It is not for nothing that he never wants to speak.
The one thing he wants is to learn mother's words
from mother's lips.
That is why he looks so innocent.

Baby had a heap of gold and pearls,
yet he came like a beggar onto this earth.
It is not for nothing he came in such a disguise.
This dear little naked mendicant pretends to be
utterly helpless,
so that he may beg for mother's wealth of love.

Baby was so free from every tie in the land of
the tiny crescent moon.
It was not for nothing he gave up his freedom.
He knows that there is room for endless joy in
mother's little corner of a heart,
and it is sweeter far than liberty to be caught
and pressed in her dear arms.

Baby never knew how to cry.
He dwelt in the land of perfect bliss.
It is not for nothing he has chosen to shed
tears.
Though with the smile of his dear face he
draws mother's yearning heart to him,
yet his little cries over tiny troubles weave the
double bond of pity and love.

THE UNHEEDED PAGEANT

Ah, who was it colored that little frock, my child, and covered your sweet limbs with that little red tunic?

You have come out in the morning to play in the courtyard, tottering and tumbling as you run.

But who was it colored that little frock, my child?

What is it makes you laugh, my little life—bud?

Mother smiles at you standing on the threshold.

She claps her hands and her bracelets jingle,

and you dance with your bamboo stick in your hand like a tiny little shepherd.

But what is it makes you laugh, my little life—bud?

O beggar, what do you beg for,

clinging to your mother's neck with both your hands?

O greedy heart,

shall I pluck the world like a fruit from the sky to place it on your little rosy palm?

O beggar, what are you begging for?

The wind carries away in glee the tinkling of your anklet bells.

The sun smiles and watches your toilet.

The sky watches over you when you sleep in your mother's arms,

and the morning tiptoes to your bed and kisses your eyes.

The wind carries away in glee the tinkling of your anklet bells.

The fairy mistress of dreams is coming towards you, flying through the twilight sky.

The world—mother keeps her seat by you in your mother's heart.

He who plays his music to the stars is standing at your window with his flute.

And the fairy mistress of dreams is coming towards you, flying through the twilight sky.

SLEEP—STEALER

Who stole sleep from baby's eyes?

I must know.

Clasping her pitcher to her waist mother went to fetch water from

the village nearby.

It was noon.

The children's playtime was over;

the ducks in the pond were silent.

The shepherd boy lay asleep under the shadow of the banyan tree.

The crane stood grave and still in the swamp near the mango

grove.

In the meanwhile the sleep—stealer came and,

snatching sleep from baby's eyes,

flew away.

When mother came back she found baby traveling the room over

on all fours.

Who stole sleep from our baby's eyes?

I must know.

I must find her and chain her up.

I must look into that dark cave,

where,

through boulders and scowling stones,

trickles a tiny stream.

I must search in the drowsy shade of the bakula grove,

where pigeons coo in their corner,

and fairies' anklets tinkle in the stillness of starry nights.

In the evening I will peep into the whispering silence of the bamboo forest,

 where fireflies squander their light,

and will ask every creature I meet,

"Can anybody tell me where the sleep—stealer lives?"

Who stole sleep from baby's eyes?

I must know.

Shouldn't I give her a good lesson if I could only catch her!

I would raid her nest and see where she hoards all her stolen sleep.

I would plunder it all,

and carry it home.

I would bind her two wings securely,

set her on the bank of the river,

and then let her play at fishing with a reed among the

rushes and water—lilies.

When the marketing is over in the evening,

and the village children sit in their mothers' laps, then the

night birds will mockingly din her ears with:

"whose sleep will you steal now?"

THE BEGINNING

"Where have I come from, where did you pick me up?"
The baby asked its mother.She answered half crying,
half laughing,
and clasping the baby to her breast,
You were hidden in my heart as its desire, my darling.
You were in the dolls of my childhood's games;
and when with clay I made the image of my god every
morning, I made and unmade you then.
You were enshrined with our household deity,
in his worship I worshipped you.

In all my hopes and my loves,
in my life,
in the life of my mother you have lived.
In the lap of the deathless spirit who rules our home you have
been nursed for ages.
When in girlhood my heart was opening its petals,
you hovered as a fragrance about it.
Your tender softness bloomed in my youthful limbs,

like a glow in the sky before the sunrise.
Heaven's first darling,
twin—born with the morning light,
you have floated down the stream of the
world's life and at last you have stranded on
my heart.

As I gaze on your face,
mystery overwhelms me;
you who belong to all have become mine.
For fear of losing you I hold you tight to my
breast.
What magic has snared the world's treasure in
these slender arms of mine?

BABY'S WORLD

I wish I could take a quiet corner in the heart of my baby's very own world.

I know it has stars that talk to him,

and a sky that stoops down to his face to amuse him with its silly clouds and rainbows.

Those who make believe to be dumb,

and look as if they never could move,

come creeping to his window with their stories and with trays crowded with bright toys.

I wish I could travel by the road that crosses baby's mind,

and out beyond all bounds;

Where messengers run errands for no cause between the kingdoms of kings of no history;

Where Reason makes kites of the laws and flies them,

and Truth sets Fact free from its fetters.

WHEN AND WHY

When I bring you colored toys,

my child.

I understand why there is such a play of colors on

clouds, on water,

and why flowers are painted in tints—when I give

colored toys to you, my child.

When I sing to make you dance,

I truly know why there is music in leaves,

and why waves send their chorus of voices to the

heart of the listening earth—when I sing to make

you dance.

When I bring sweet things to your greedy hands,

I know why there is honey in the cup of the flower,

and why fruits are secretly filled with sweet juice—

when I bring sweet things to your greedy hands.

When I kiss your face to make you smile,

my darling,

I surely understand what pleasure streams

from the sky in morning light,

and what delight the summer breeze brings

to my body—when I kiss you to make you

smile.

DEFAMATION

Why are those tears in your eyes, my child?

How horrid of them to be always scolding you for nothing?

You have stained your fingers and face with ink while writing—is that why they call you dirty?

O, fie!

would they dare to call the full moon dirty because it has smudged its face with ink?

For every little trifle they blame you,

my child.

They are ready to find fault for nothing.

You tore your clothes while playing—is that why they call you untidy?

O, fie!

What would they call an autumn morning that smiles through its ragged clouds?

Take no heed of what they say to you,

my child.

They make a long list of your misdeeds.

Everybody knows how you love sweet things

—is that why they call you greedy?

O, fie!

What then would they call us who love you?

THE JUDGE

Say of him what you please,
but I know my child's failings.

I do not love him because he is good,
but because he is my little child.

How should you know how dear he can be when you try to
weigh his merits against his faults?

When I must punish him he becomes all the more a part of my
being.

When I cause his tears to come my heart weeps with him.

I alone have a right to blame and punish,
for he only may chastise who loves.

PLAYTHINGS

Child,

how happy you are sitting in the dust,

playing with a broken twig all the morning.

I smile at your play with that little bit of a broken twig.

I am busy with my accounts,

adding up figures by the hour.

Perhaps you glance at me and think,

"What a stupid game to spoil your morning with!"

Child, I have forgotten the art of being absorbed in sticks and

mud—pies.

I seek out costly playthings,

and gather lumps of gold and silver.

With whatever you find you create your glad games,

I spend both my time and my strength over things I can never

obtain.

In my frail canoe I struggle to cross the sea of desire,

and forget that I too am playing a game in it.

THE ASTRONOMER

I only said,

"When in the evening the round full moon gets entangled
among the branches of that Kadam tree, couldn't
somebody catch it?"

But dada (elder brother) laughed at me and said,
"Baby, you are the silliest child I have ever known.
The moon is ever so far from us, how could anybody
catch it?"

I said, "Dada, how foolish you are!
When mother looks out of her window and smiles down
at us playing,
would you call her far away?"
Still dada said, "You are a stupid child!
But, baby, where could you find a net big enough to
catch the moon with?"
I said, "Surely you could catch it with your hands."
But dada laughed and said,

"You are the silliest child I have known.
If it came nearer,
you would see how big the moon is."

I said, "Dada, what nonsense they teach at
your school!
When mother bends her face down to kiss us
does her face look very big?"
But still dada says,
"You are a stupid child."

CLOUDS AND WAVES

Mother,

the folk who live up in the clouds call out to me —

"We play from the time we wake till the day ends.

We play with the golden dawn,

we play with the silver moon."

I ask, "But, how am I to get up to you?"

They answer,

"Come to the edge of the earth,

lift up your hands to the sky,

and you will be taken up into the clouds."

"My mother is waiting for me at home,"

I say,

"How can I leave her and come?"

Then they smile and float away.

But I know a nicer game than that, mother.

I shall be the cloud and you the moon.

I shall cover you with both my hands,

and our housetop will be the blue sky.

The folk who live in the waves call out to me —

"We sing from morning till night;

on and on we travel and know not where we

pass."

I ask, "But, how am I to join you?"

They tell me,

"Come to the edge of the shore and stand with

your eyes tight shut and you will be carried out

upon the waves."

I say, "My mother always wants me at home in

the evening—how can I leave her and go?"

Then they smile, dance and pass by.

But I know a better game than that.

I will be the waves and you will be a strange

shore.

I shall roll on and on,

and break upon your lap with laughter.

And no one in the world will know where we

both are.

THE CHAMPA FLOWER

Supposing I became a champa flower,

just for fun,

and grew on a branch high up that tree,

and shook in the wind with laughter and danced

upon the newly budded leaves,

would you know me, mother?

You would call, "Baby, where are you?"

and I should laugh to myself and keep quite quiet.

I should slyly open my petals and watch you at your

work.

When after your bath,

with wet hair spread on your shoulders,

you walked through the shadow of the champa tree

to the little court where you say your prayers,

you would notice the scent of the flower,

but not know that it came from me.

When after the midday meal you sat at the window

reading Ramayana,

and the tree's shadow fell over your hair and

your lap,

I should fling my wee little shadow on to the

page of your book, just where you were reading.

But would you guess that it was the tiny shadow

of your little child?

When in the evening you went to the cowshed

with the lighted lamp in your hand,

I should suddenly drop on to the earth again and

be your own baby once more,

and beg you to tell me a story.

"Where have you been, you naughty child?"

"I won't tell you, mother."

That's what you and I would say then.

FAIRYLAND

If people came to know where my king's palace is,

it would vanish into the air.

The walls are of white silver and the roof of shining gold.

The queen lives in a palace with seven courtyards,

and she wears a jewel that cost all the wealth of seven

kingdoms.

But let me tell you, mother, in a whisper,

where my king's palace is.

It is at the corner of our terrace where the pot of the

tulsi plant stands.

The princess lies sleeping on the far—away shore of the

seven impassable seas.

There is none in the world who can find her but myself.

She has bracelets on her arms and pearl drops in her

ears;

her hair sweeps down upon the floor.

She will wake when I touch her with my magic wand,

and jewels will fall from her lips when she smiles.

But let me whisper in your ear, mother;

she is there in the corner of our terrace where the

pot of the tulsi plant stands.

When it is time for you to go to the river for your

bath, step up to that terrace on the roof.

I sit in the corner where the shadows of the walls

meet together.

Only puss is allowed to come with me,

for she knows where the barber in the story lives.

But let me whisper,

mother, in your ear where the barber in the story

lives.

It is at the corner of the terrace where the pot of the

tulsi plant stands.

THE LAND OF THE EXILE

Mother, the light has grown grey in the sky;

I do not know what the time is.

There is no fun in my play,

so I have come to you.

It is Saturday, our holiday.

Leave off your work, mother;

sit here by the window and tell me where the desert of Tepantar in the fairy tale is.

The shadow of the rains has covered the day from end to end.

The fierce lightning is scratching the sky with its nails.

When the clouds rumble and it thunders,

I love to be afraid in my heart and cling to you.

When the heavy rain patters for hours on the bamboo leaves,

and our windows shake and rattle at the gusts of wind,

I like to sit alone in the room,

mother, with you,

and hear you talk about the desert of Tepantar in the fairy tale.

Where is it,

mother, on the shore of what sea,

at the foot of what hills,

in the kingdom of what king?

There are no hedges there to mark the fields,

no footpath across it by which the villages reach their village in

the evening,

or the woman who gathers dry sticks in the forest can bring her

load to the market.

With patches of yellow grass in the sand and only one tree

where the pair of wise old birds have their nest,

lies the desert of Tepantar.

I can imagine how, on just such a cloudy day,

the young son of the king is riding alone on a grey horse through

the desert,

in search of the princess who lies imprisoned in the giant's palace

across that unknown water.

When the haze of the rain comes down in the distant sky,

and lightning starts up like a sudden fit of pain,

does he remember his unhappy mother,

abandoned by the king,

sweeping the cow—stall and wiping her eyes,

while he rides through the desert of Tepantar in the fairytale?

See, mother, it is almost dark before the day is over,

and there are no travellers yonder on the village road.

The shepherd boy has gone home early from the pasture,

and men have left their fields to sit on mats under the eaves of

their huts, watching the scowling clouds.

Mother,

I have left all my books on the shelf — do not ask me to do my lessons now.

When I grow up and am big like my father,

I shall learn all that must be learnt.

But just for today, tell me, mother,

where the desert of Tepantar in the fairy tale is?

THE RAINY DAY

Sullen clouds are gathering fast over the black fringe of the forest.

O child, do not go out!

The palm trees in a row by the lake are smiting their heads against the dismal sky;

the crows with their draggled wings are silent on the tamarind branches,

and the eastern back of the river is haunted by deepening gloom.

Our cow is owing loud, tied at the fence.

O child, wait here till I bring her into the stall.

Men have crowed into flooded field to catch the fishes as they escape from the over lowing ponds;

the rain—water is running in rills through the narrow lanes like a laughing boy who has run away from his mother to tease her.

Listen, someone is shouting for the boatman at the ford.

O child, the daylight is dim, and the crossing at the ferry is closed.

The sky seems to ride fast upon the madly— rushing rain;

the water in the river is loud and impatient;

women have hastened home early from the Ganges with their filled pitchers.

The evening lamps must be made ready.

O child, do not go out!

The road to the market is desolate,

the lane to the river is slippery.

The wind is roaring and struggling among the bamboo branches like a wild beast tangled in a net.

PAPER BOATS

Day by day I float my paper boats one by one down the running stream.

In big black letters I write my name on them and the name of the village where I live.

I hope that someone in some strange land will find them and know who I am.

I load my little boats with shiuli flowers from our garden,

and hope that these blooms of the dawn will be carried safely to land in the night.

I launch my paper boats and look up into the sky and see the little clouds setting their white bulging sails.

I know not what playmate of mine in the sky sends them down the air to race with my boats!

When night comes I bury my face in my arms and dream that my paper boats float on and on under the midnight stars.

The fairies of sleep are sailing in them,

and the lading is their baskets full of dreams.

THE SAILOR

The boat of the boatman Madhu is moored at the
wharf of Rajgunj.
It is uselessly laden with jute,
and has been lying there idle for ever so long.
If he would only lend me his boat,
I should man her with a hundred oars,
and hoist sails, five or six or seven.
I should never steer her to stupid markets.

I should sail the seven seas and the thirteen rivers of
fairyland.
But, mother,
you won't weep for me in a corner.
I am not going into the forest like Ramachandra to
come back only after fourteen years.

I shall become the prince of the story,
and fill my boat with whatever I like.
I shall take my friend Ashu with me.

We shall sail merrily across the seven seas and
the thirteen rivers of fairyland.
We shall set sail in the early morning light.
When at noontide you are bathing at the
pond,
we shall be in the land of a strange king.
We shall pass the shallous of Tirpurni,
and leave behind us the desert of Tepantar.

When we come back it will be getting dark,
and I shall tell you of all that we have seen.
I shall cross the seven seas and the thirteen
rivers of fairyland.

THE FURTHER BANK

I LONG to go over there to the further bank of the river.

Where those boats are tied to the bamboo poles in a line;

Where men cross over in their boats in the morning with ploughs on
their shoulders to till their far—away fields;

Where the cowherds make their lowing cattle swim across to the
riverside pasture;

Evenfall they all come back home in the evening,

leaing the jackals to howl in the island overgrown with weeds.

Mother, if you don't mind,

I should like to become the boatman of the ferryboat when I am
grown up.

They say there are strange pools hidden behind that high bank.

Where flocks of wild ducks come when the rains are over,

and thick reeds grow round the margins where water—birds lay their
eggs;

Where snipes with their dancing tails stamp their tiny footprints upon
the clean soft mud;

Where in the evening the tall grasses crested with white flowers invite the
moonbeam to float upon their waves.
Mother, if you don't mind,
I should like to become the boatman of the ferryboat when I am grown up.

I shall cross and cross back from bank to bank,
and all the boys and girls of the village will wonder at me while they are
bathing.
When the sun climbs the mid sky and morning wears onto noon,
I shall come running to you, saying,
"Mother, I am hungry!"
When the day is done and the shadows cower under the trees,
I shall come back in the dusk.
I shall never go away from you into the town to work like father.
Mother, if you don't mind,
I should like to become the boatman of the ferryboat when I am grown up.

THE FLOWER-SCHOOL

When storm clouds rumble in the sky and June showers
come down.

The moist east wind comes marching over the heath to
blow its bag-pipes among the bamboos.

Then crowds of flowers come out of a sudden,

from nobody knows where,

and dance upon the grass in wild glee.

Mother,

I really think the flowers go to school underground.

They do their lessons with doors shut,

and if they want to come out to play before it is time,

their master makes them stand in a corner.

When the rains come they have their holidays.

Branches clash together in the forest,

and the leaves rustle in the wild wind,

 the thunder-clouds clap their giant hands and the flower
children rush out in dresses of pink and yellow and white.

Do you know,

mother, their home is in the sky,

where the stars are.

Haven't you seen how eager they are to
get there?

Don't you know why they are in such a
hurry?

Of course, I can guess to whom they raise
their arms:

they have their mother as I have my own.

THE MERCHANT

Imagine, mother,
that you are to stay at home and I am to travel
into strange lands.
Imagine that my boat is ready at the landing
fully laden.
Now think well,
mother, before you say what I shall bring for
you when I come back.

Mother, do you want heaps and heaps of gold?
There, by the banks of golden streams,
fields are full of golden harvest.
And in the shade of the forest path the golden
champa flowers drop on the ground.
I will gather them all for you in many hundred
baskets.

Mother,
do you want pearls big as the raindrops of
autumn?
I shall cross to the pearl island shore.
There in the early morning light pearls
tremble on the meadow flowers,
pearls drop on the grass,
and pearls are scattered on the sand in spray
by the wild sea-waves.
My brother shall have a pair of horses with
wings to fly among the clouds.
For father I shall bring a magic pen that,
without his knowing, will write of itself.
For you, mother,
I must have the casket and jewel that cost
seven kings their kingdoms.

SYMPATHY

If I were only a little puppy,

not your baby, mother dear,

would you say "No" to me if I tried to eat from your dish?

Would you drive me off,

saying to me, "Get away, you naughty little puppy."

Then go, mother,

go! I will never come to you when you call me,

and never let you feed me any more.

If I were only a little green parrot,

and not your baby, mother dear,

would you keep me chained lest I should fly away?

Would you shake your finger at me and say,

"What an ungrateful wretch of a bird!

It is gnawing at its chain day and night?"

Then, go, mother, go!

I will run away into the woods,

I will never let you take me in your arms again.

114

VOCATION

When the gong sounds ten in the morning and I

walk to school by our lane.

Every day I meet the hawker crying,

"Bangles, crystal bangles!"

There is nothing to hurry him on,

there is no road he must take,

no place he must go to,

no time when he must come home.

I wish I were a hawker,

spending my day in the road,

crying, "Bangles, crystal bangles!"

When at four in the afternoon I come back from

the school.

I can see through the gate of that house the

gardener digging the ground.

He does what he likes with his spade,

he soils his clothes with dust,

nobody takes him to task if he gets baked in the

sun or gets wet.

I wish I were a gardener digging away at the

garden with nobody to stop me from digging.

Just as it gets dark in the evening and my

mother sends me to bed.

I can see through my open window the

watchman walking up and down.

The lane is dark and lonely,

and the street-lamp stands like a giant with

one red eye in its head.

The watchman swings his lantern and walks

with his shadow at his side,

and never once goes to bed in his life.

I wish I were a watchman walking the streets all

night,

chasing the shadows with my lantern.

SUPERIOR

Mother, your baby is silly!
She is so absurdly childish!

She does not know the difference between the
lights in the streets and the stars.

When we play at eating with pebbles,
she thinks they are real food,
and tries to put them into her mouth.

When I open a book before her and ask her to
learn her a,b,c,
she tears the leaves with her hands and roars for
joy at nothing; this is your baby's way of doing her
lesson.

When I shake my head at her in anger and scold
her and call her naughty,
she laughs and thinks it great fun.

Everybody knows that father is away,
but if in play I call aloud "Father,"
she looks about her in excitement and thinks
that father is near.

When I hold my class with the donkeys that our
washerman brings to carry away the clothes
and I warn her that I am the schoolmaster,
she will scream for no reason and call me dada
(elder brother).

Your baby wants to catch the moon.
She is so funny; she calls Ganesh Ganush.
Mother, your baby is silly,
she is so absurdly childish!

THE LITTLE BIG MAN

I am small because I am a little child.

I shall be big when I am as old as my father is.

My teacher will come and say,

"It is late, bring your slate and your books."

I shall tell him,

"Do you not know I am as big as father?

And I must not have lessons any more."

My master will wonder and say,

"He can leave his books if he likes, for he is grown up."

I shall dress myself and walk to the fair where the crowd is thick.

My uncle will come rushing up to me and say,

"You will get lost, my boy; let me carry you."

I shall answer,

"Can't you see, uncle, I am as big as father,

I must go to the fair alone."

Uncle will say,

"Yes, he can go wherever he likes, for he is grown up."

Mother will come from her bath when I am giving money to my nurse, for I shall know how to open the box with my key.

Mother will say,

"What are you about, naughty child?"

I shall tell her, "Mother, don't you know,

I am as big as father,

and I must give silver to my nurse."

Mother will say to herself,

"He can give money to whom he likes,

for he is grown up."

In the holiday time in October father will come home and,

thinking that I am still a baby,

will bring for me from the town little shoes and small silken

frocks.

I shall say, "Father, give them to my dada (elder brother),

for I am as big as you are."

Father will think and say,

"He can buy his own clothes if he likes, for he

is grown up."

TWELVE O'CLOCK

Mother, I do want to leave off my lessons now.
I have been at my book all the morning.

You say it is only twelve o'clock.
Suppose it isn't any later;
can't you ever think it is afternoon when it is only twelve o'clock?

I can easily imagine now that the sun has reached the edge of that rice—field,
and the old fisher—woman is gathering herbs for her supper by the side of the
pond.

I can just shut my eyes and think that the shadows are growing darker under
the madar tree,
and the water in the pond looks shiny black.
If twelve o'clock can come in the night,
why can't the night come when it is twelve o'clock?

AUTHORSHIP

You say that father writes a lot of books,
but what he writes I don't understand.

He was reading to you all the evening,
but could you really make out what he meant?

What nice stories, mother,
you can tell us! Why can't father write like that,
I wonder?

Did he never hear from his own mother stories of giants and
fairies and princesses?

Has he forgotten them all?
Often when he gets late for his bath you have to go and call him
an hundred times.

You wait and keep his dishes warm for him,
but he goes on writing and forgets.

Father always play at making books.

If ever I go to play in father's room,

you come and call me, "What a naughty child!"

If I make the slightest noise,

you say,

Don't you see that father's at his work?"

What's the fun of always writing and writing?

When I take up father's pen or pencil and write upon his book

just as he does ,

— a, b, c, d, e, f, g, h, i...

Why do you get cross with me then mother?

You never say a word when father writes.

When my father wastes such heaps of paper,

mother,you don't seem to mind at all.

But if I take only one sheet to make a boat with,

you say,"Child, how troublesome you are!"

What do you think of father's spoiling sheets and sheets of paper

with black marks all over on both sides?

THE WICKED POSTMAN

Why do you sit there on the floor so quiet and silent,

tell me, mother dear?

The rain is coming in through the open window,

making you all wet, and you don't mind it.

Do you hear the gong striking four?

It is time for my brother to come home from school.

What has happened to you that you look so strange?

Haven't you got a letter from father today?

I saw the postman bringing letters in his bag for almost

everybody in the town.

Only, father's letters he keeps to read himself.

I am sure the postman is a wicked man.

But don't be unhappy about that,

mother dear.

Tomorrow is market day in the next village.

You ask your maid to buy some pens and papers.

I myself will write all father's letters;

you will not find a single mistake.

I shall write from A right up to K.

But, mother, why do you smile?

You don't believe that I can write as nicely as father does!

But I shall rule my paper carefully,

and write all the letters beautifully big.

When I finish my writing,

do you think I shall be so foolish as father and drop it into

the horrid postman's bag?

I shall bring it to you myself without waiting,

and letter by letter help you to read my writing.

I know the postman does not like to give you the really nice

letters.

THE HERO

Mother, let us imagine we are travelling,

and passing through a strange and dangerous country.

You are riding in a palanquin and I am trotting by you on a red

horse.

It is evening and the sun goes down.

The waste of Joradighi lies wan and grey before us.

The land is desolate and barren.

You are frightened and thinking —

"I know not where we have come to."

I say to you, "Mother, do not be afraid."

The meadow is prickly with spiky grass,

and through it runs a narrow broken path.

There are no cattle to be seen in the wide field;

they have gone to their village stalls.

It grows dark and dim on the land and sky,

and we cannot tell where we are going.

Suddenly you call me and ask me in a whisper,

"What light is that near the bank?"

Just then there bursts out a fearful yell,

and figures come running towards us.

You sit crouched in your palanquin and repeat the names of the gods in prayer.

The bearers, shaking in terror,

hide themselves in the thorny bush.

I shout to you, "Don't be afraid, mother, I am here."

With long sticks in their hands and hair all wild about their heads,

they come nearer and nearer.

I shout, "Have a care! you villains!

One step more and you are dead men."

They give another terrible yell and rush forward.

You clutch my hand and say,

"Dear boy, for heaven's sake, keep away from them."

I say, "Mother, just you watch me."

Then I spur my horse for a wild gallop,

and my sword and buckler clash against each other.

The fight becomes so fearful,

mother,

that it would give you a cold shudder could you see it from your palanquin.

Many of them fly,

and a great number are cut to pieces.

I know you are thinking,

sitting all by yourself,

that your boy must be dead by this time.

But I come to you all stained with blood,

and say, "Mother, the fight is over now."

You come out and kiss me, pressing me to your heart, and you say to yourself,

"I don't know what I should do if I hadn't my boy to escort me."

A thousand useless things happen day after day,

and why couldn't such a thing come true by chance?

It would be like a story in a book.

My brother would say, "Is it possible?

I always thought he was so delicate!"

Our village people would all say in amazement,

"Was it not lucky that the boy was with his mother?"

THE END

It is time for me to go,

mother; I am going.

When in the paling darkness of the lonely dawn you stretch out

your arms for your baby in the bed,

I shall say, "Baby is not there!"

— Mother, I am going.

I shall become a delicate draught of air and caress you;

and I shall be ripples in the water when you bathe,

and kiss you and kiss you again.

In the gusty night when the rain patters on the leaves you will

hear my whisper in your bed,

and my laughter will flash with the lightning through the open

window into your room.

If you lie awake,

thinking of your baby till late into the night,

I shall sing to you from the stars,

"Sleep! mother, sleep."

On the straying moonbeams I shall steal over your bed,

and lie upon your bosom while you sleep.

I shall become a dream,

and through the little opening of your eyelids I shall slip into the depths of your sleep;

and when you wake up and look round startled,

like a twinkling firefly I shall flit out into the darkness.

When, on the great festival of puja,

the neighbours' children come and play about the house.

I shall melt into the music of the flute and throb in your heart all day.

Dear auntie will come with puja—presents and will ask,

"Where is our baby, sister?"

Mother, you will tell her softly,

"He is in the pupils of my eyes, he is in my body and in my soul."

THE RECALL

The night was dark when she went away,

and they slept.

The night is dark now,

and I call for her,

"Come back,

my darling;

the world is asleep;

and no one would know,

if you came for a moment while stars are gazing

at stars."

She went away when the trees were in bud and

the spring was young.

Now the flowers are in high bloom and I call,

"Come back, my darling.

The children gather and scatter flowers in reckless

sport.

And if you come and take one little blossom no

one will miss it."

Those that used to play are playing still,

so spendthrift is life.

I listen to their chatter and call,

"Come back, my darling, for mother's heart

is full to the brim with love,

and if you come to snatch only one little

kiss from her no one will grudge it."

THE FIRST JASMINES

All, these jasmines,
these white jasmines!

I seem to remember the first day when I filled my
hands with these jasmines,
these white jasmines.

I have loved the sunlight,
the sky and the green earth;
I have heard the liquid murmur of the river
through the darkness of midnight;
Autumn sunsets have come to me at the bend of a
road in the lonely waste,
like a bride raising her veil to accept her lover.

Yet my memory is still sweet with the first white
jasmines that
I held in my hand when I was a child.

Many a glad day has come in my life,
and I have laughed with merrymakers on
festival nights.

On grey mornings of rain I have crooned
many an idle song.

I have worn round my neck the evening
wreath of bakulas woven by the hand of
love.

Yet my heart is sweet with the memory of
the first fresh jasmines that filled my hands
when I was a child.

THE BANYAN TREE

O you shaggy—headed banyan tree standing
on the bank of the pond,
have you forgotten the little child,
like the birds that have nested in your branches
and left you?

Do you not remember how he sat at the
window and wondered at the tangle of your
roots that plunged underground?

The women would come to fill their jars in
the pond, and your huge black shadow would
wriggle on the water like sleep struggling to
wake up.

Sunlight danced on the ripples like restless tiny
shuttles weaving golden tapestry.
Two ducks swam by weedy margin above their
shadows,
and the child would sit still and think.

He longed to be the wind and blow through your
rustling branches,
to be your shadow and lengthen with the day on the
water,
to be a bird and perch on your topmost twig,
and to float like those ducks among the weeds and
shadows.

BENEDICTION

Bless this little heart,

this white soul that has won the kiss of heaven

for our earth.

He loves the light of the sun,

he loves the sight of his mother's face.

He has not learned to despise the dust,

and to hanker after gold.

Clasp him to your heart and bless him.

He has come into this land of an hundred cross—

roads.

I know not how he chose you from the crowd,

came to your door,

and grasped your hand to ask his way.

He will follow you, laughing and talking,

and not a doubt in his heart.

Keep his trust,

lead him straight and bless him.

Lay your hand on his head,

and pray that though the waves underneath

grow threatening,

yet the breath from above may come and fill

his sails and waft him to the haven of peace.

Forget him not in your hurry,

let him come to your heart and bless him.

THE GIFT

I want to give you something,

my child, for we are drifting in the stream of the world.

Our lives will be carried apart, and our love forgotten.

But I am not so foolish as to hope that I could buy your heart with my gifts.

Young is your life, your path long,

and you drink the love we bring you at one draught and turn and run away from us.

You have your play and your playmates.

What harm is there if you have no time or thought for us?

We, indeed,

have leisure enough in old age to count the days that are past,

to cherish in our hearts what our hands have lost for ever.

The river runs swift with a song, breaking through all barriers.

But the mountain stays and remembers,

and follows her with his love.

MY SONG

This song of mine will wind its music around you,

my child, like the fond arms of love.

This song of mine will touch your forehead like a kiss of blessing.

When you are alone it will sit by your side ang whisper in your ear,

when you are in the crowd it will fence you about with aloofness.

My song will be like a pair of wings to your dreams,

it will transport your heart to the verge of the unknown.

It will be like the faithful star overhead when dark night is over your road.

My song will sit in the pupils of your eyes,

and will carry your sight into the heart of things.

And when my voice is silenced in death,

my song will speak in your living heart.

THE CHILD—ANGEL

They clamour and fight,

they doubt and despair,

they know no end to their wranglings.

Let your life come amongst them like a flame of light,

my child, unflickering and pure,

and delight them into silence.

They are cruel in their greed and their envy,

their words are like hidden knives thirsting for blood.

Go and stand amidst their scowling hearts,

my child, and let your gentle eyes fall upon them like

the forgiving peace of the evening over the strife of the

day.

Let them see your face,

my child, and thus know the meaning of all things;

let them love you and thus love each other.

Come and take your seat in the bosom of the limitless,

my child.

At sunrise open and raise your heart like a

blossoming flower,

and at sunset bend your head and in silence

complete the worship of the day.

THE LAST BARGAIN

"Come and hire me! "I cried, while in the morning I was
walking on the stone—paved road.
Sword in hand, the King came in his chariot.
He held my hand and said, "I will hire you with my
power."
But his power counted for nought, and he went away in
his chariot.

In the heat of the midday the houses stood with shut
doors.

I wandered along the crooked lane.
An old man came out with his bag of gold.

He pondered and said, "I will hire you with my money."
He weighed his coins one by one,but I turned away.
It was evening.The garden hedge was all a flower.
The fair maid came out and said,
"I will hire you with a smile."

Her smile paled and melted into tears,
and she went back alone into the dark.

The sun glistened on the sand,
and the sea waves broke waywardly.

A child sat playing with shells.

He raised his head and seemed to know me,
and said, "I hire you with nothing."

From thence forward that bargain struck in
child's play made me a free man.